Fenian Brotherhood, Dept. of Manhattan

To the Fenian Brotherhood of America

official report of the Investigating Committee of the Department of

Manhattan, Fenian Brotherhood

Fenian Brotherhood, Dept. of Manhattan

To the Fenian Brotherhood of America
official report of the Investigating Committee of the Department of Manhattan,
Fenian Brotherhood

ISBN/EAN: 9783337377533

Printed in Europe, USA, Canada, Australia, Japan

Cover: Foto ©Andreas Hilbeck / pixelio.de

More available books at **www.hansebooks.com**

T O

The   Fenian   Brotherhood

Of   America

OFFICAL   REPORT

Of   The

INVESTIGATING   COMMITTEE

Of   The

DEPARTMENT   OF   MANHATTAN,

FENIAN   BROTHERHOOD

A Full And Complete   Report   Of The

Investagation   Of   The   Management

Of   Affairs,   Financial,   Military

And   Civil,   Of   Officals

At   The   Fenian   Headquarters ---

(Moffatt Mansion)   Union   Square,   N. Y.

Statement   Of   Monies   Received
And   Expended,   Bonds   Issued --
Full   History   Of   The   "CAMPO BELLO" FIZZLE.

PRICE   30   CENTS.

----   ----

New   York

----

1 8 6 6

My position in the F. B. was Secretary of Military and Naval Affairs. I held that office about three months. My staff consisted of Colonel Mulcahy, Adjutant General; Col. Murray, Chief of Artillery; Col. Kelly, Inspector-General; Captain Hodgson, Chief Clerk of Naval Department. Their salary was at a rate of $1,200 per annum. I was about to purchase two batteries and had made all the arrangements for the purchase of one of them, but could not get the money to do it. The Central Council prevented its purchase. My staff received extra compensation for services as Organizers, &c., in addition to their regular pay. I think they were of great benefit to the Brotherhood. Capt. Hodgson was not an Organizer. I do not consider it was unpatriotic for salaried officers to charge expenses of public meetings. I do not think that the F. B. could have done without my staff. No one man could have attended to the duties of my staff. There was one vessel belonging to the Naval Department of the F. B. I did not depend so much on voluntary donations of arms as on those offered for sale. I never set a particular day for moving. I expressed a hope to James Stephens that we might soon leave America with two ships, and from 10 to 20,000 stand of arms. Enfield rifles were offered at 1.25 apiece. I sent to Ireland for a signal officer. I never promised Capt. M'Cafferty that I would send Capt. Barbot or a major to Europe, nor said that I wanted Capt. Barbot to go South to look after some artillery that was concealed there.

A proposition was made to me to run the Privateer out to sea on the 17th day of March, via Jones Woods: but I demurred to that on account of Col. O'Mahony being absent from the city at the time.

Mr. B. D. Killian, when purchase of a vessel was first talked of, introduced me to Mr. Shibley, who pretended to me that he was the owner of the vessel which has been bought. Shibley first asked $40,000 for her, but was willing to take $37,500. Mr. Killian told me to buy the vessel as cheap as I possibly could. I saw Mr. Pierce Skeehan, and asked him to take the ownership of the vessel. He wanted

first to consult a lawyer - one in our interest.   I ordered him to buy the vessel.
Mr. Skeehan desiring to fee the lawyer, I granted him(Mr. Skeehan) $500 to indemnify
him against all losses of a personal character.   The vessel was bought for $29,500;
I drew a draft for 30,000.   Mr. Skeehan claimed that he had saved $500 for the
Brotherhood, stating that he had purchased her for $29,000.   Mr. Skeehan desired
to give me, and then Col. O'Mahony, this $500 balance, but we told him to tender it
to the Secretary of the Treasury, the proper party to receive it.

(The books of the F. B. show the price paid for the vessel as $30,000, whereas
she actually cost but $29,000 - the $1,000 difference not being paid back to the
Treasury.)

"I never heard of the Campo Bello movement until it took place.   The Campo
Bello or any other movements were not discussed or alluded to at the Military
Convention of which I was the chairman.   My plan was to dispatch one vessel to the
north, commanded by myself, to the north of Ireland, and the H. C. was to go to
another point in Ireland in a second vessel both to be supplied with plenty of arms.

"Why my plan for a direct movement on Ireland never succeeded, I cannot tell.
There seemed to be an unseen power thwarting every plan.   I heard it stated that
the Central Council was to be considered as the great military body of F. B.   Mr.
Kavanagh was opposed to the scheme unless the Central Council ordered and controlled
it.   Mr. Sinnott was opposed to my plan.   My opinion was, and is that the Central
Council was opposed to any movement toward Ireland.   I sent in a requisition for
$89,000 to carry out this plan, but I never heard from it again.

"Mr. Killian tried to be Secretary of War as well as Secretary of the Treasury.
The 'Central Council' also tried their hands at military matters.   I then sent in my
resignation as Secretary of War of the F. B."

General Mullen here presented to Committee a copy of his letter of resignation:

"Fenian Brotherhood
"Headquarters Expeditionary Bureau
" 32 E. 17th St., Union Square
"N.Y. City, March 31, 1866

"Col. John O'Mahony, H. C. F. B.,

"Dear Sir: In order to place myself right in your estimation and to justify

my resignation as Secretary of Military and Naval Affairs of the F. B.   I beg to sub-

mit the following facts:

"You know better than any other officer at headquarters that my personal affairs,

financially, are, and have been for some time in an unsettled and dangerous condition.

"This of itself would justify my resigning the very honorable and responsible

position I hold in the Brotherhood; but in addition to this, while I am willing to

make some sacrifices, there have been of late causes of an official character that

obliges me to resign the trust of office you so kindly bestowed on me.   These causes

I will now present to you:

"1st.   There has been an intermeddling in the affairs of the department I have

the honor to supervise by the head of another department.   Officers under my control

have been ordered to a special duty without consulting me, thus assuring such officers

that I had not the control of my own affairs, and weakning my authority, to the

detriment of the service and the loss of my own official standing and dignity.

"2d.   The Central Council have assumed powers not granted to them by the Consti-

tution, as I shall attempt to show.   The Council by its action claims that it is a

legislative body, and at the same time a quasi Executive Council.   It has passed

laws, rules and regulations for this department.   It has even passed certain resolu-

tions instructing me in the details of office, thus attempting to usurp my functions

and judgement without releasing me from the responsibility of my position.   It has

created one of its own members, by a resolution, a member of my department without

my consent; the object of which was either to aid my inexperience, or to watch over

my honesty.   It has held star-chamber inquiries on my conduct by having brought

before it my staff officers to testify in my case without me being present, which,

but for a confidence reposed in me by the gallant and accomplished soldiers of my staff, would have begotten distrust and insubordination.   It has assumed itself the full powers of a military council and directing - to plan campaigns, direct details of the military and naval departments - instead of confining its functions to the adjudication of 'all questions pertaining to crimes and misdemeaners of persons attached to the military or naval service,' as the Constitution of the F. B. provides (Article II, Sec. 12.)   They have failed to make appropriations for my department as recommended by me, to any extent so far as my information goes; on the contrary, they hold that all matters and things required by my department must be submitted to them for approval — even to the printing of my orders and circulars I was informed should go before the Council's 'Printing Committee' for their sanction and approval.

"As every officer should justify his position by facts, let us enquire how much authority and what are the duties of the Central Council under the Constitution. Article II, Sec. 12 provides for the creation of the C. C., and clearly defines, as I have previously shown, its duties as a 'military board.'   Sec. 13th conveniently places the Council 'in perpetual session' in order to allow it 'to adjourn from time to time' that _its organization might remain in tact during adjournment_ - it may meet in perpetual session - _not sit_ in perpetual session.

"Sec. 15.   The Council shall originate 'all _propositions_ on the salaries of the Brotherhood.   Sec. 16.   The record of the voting shall be recorded, in the case reffered to in Sec. 15.

"Sec. 18.   The Council shall approve or disapprove on appropriations made by the H. C., except 'remittances to I. R. salaries and secret service.   Article III. Sec. 1, vests all Executive power in the H. C. and not in the C. C.; just as Article 1, Sec. 1. vests all legislative power in the Congress.   Section 5. Council approves or rejects nominations of Heads of Departments subject to condition in case of dis-agreement between H. C. and C. C.   Sec. 6. Provides the duties of the Council in appointing envoys, officers, etc.   Sec. 12, makes it the duty of the Central Council to examine the books of the departments and bureaus, thus creating a Committee of

Examination into 'the receipts and disbursements of each department.'

"Now, Mr. Head Centre, there is the entire duties of the Central Council as prescribed by the Constitution, the highest law known to the Brotherhood. If there are other powers given them that can affect the position I have taken, I have failed to discover them. So much for the action of the Council. Now permit me to explain my situation in another point of view. Orders after orders have been given to certain parties to do and to act — such doings and actions greatly affecting my department, and treating me as a man of straw,' and leaving the outside world to believe I am for non action, while some of my Fenian colleagues have charged me with acting too fast. Today orders were given certain Centres of Circles to have their men ready for active service in forty-eight hours. Pray for what? For another spasm? Am I to be responsible for these 'spasmodic actions?' Mr. Centre, do you know the condition at present of the vessel? A target for artillery pratice could not be more successfully painted -- black hull and straw-colored wheel-house. Some buckets were furnished that have light brass or copper handles; the first dash over the bucket is lost - the rope in the man's hand. Her rigging is in miserable condition; her sails in a worse. Doubtless full of bilgewater. Her bilge should be pumpted out and white-washed.

"She had, when last heard from by me, no hammocks, no cooking utensils, in fact, a mere shell. Her machinery and steam generating power untested; coal-bunkers and magazines empty. Seriously, is it intended to put this 'shell upon the ocean as the representative of the Fenian Navy,' and I the 'Secretary of Naval Affairs?' I hope not.

"I earnestly insist that I should have received my orders from you regarding what was to be done, and then to have had those orders carried out to the letter by officers under me. When a man serves the dearest affections, and offers his fortune and his life in a political cause, he is entitled to the respect of mankind - his opinions should be respected by his confrees. It is my duty to say now, in a

solemn manner, that calm judgement, a firm purpose, and a prudential action is required just at this time. My advice may be unheeded, yet it is my duty to give it. I have known Councellors, Senates and Central Councils before in the Brotherhood I gave advice at these periods that was unheeded; I must respectfully offer it again. In my opinion no movement should be made of a military character unless the project was submitted to the best military talent in the reach of the Brotherhood.

"The members of my Staff are as devoted to the cause of Ireland as any set of men alive. They are soldiers of pratical experience, and men of splendid courage.

"Why not submit military movements for their opinion? Can it possibly do harm? These are questions I put for a calm reflection.

"From all the foregoing you see how -- impossible it is for me to act in my present position any longer with credit to myself or benefit to the cause, therefore I respectfully insist upon the acceptance of my resignation.

"With the highest respect and esteem, I remain,

"Faithfully and fraternally, yours,

"B. F. MULLEN."

GENERAL MULLEN'S EXAMINATION RESUMED.

I remember writing a note to Col. O'Mahony in which I said: "You have been sold." I meant by that, you have listened to the advice of civilians instead of me. I know that Col. O'Mahony was opposed to the Campo Bello movement; so was Mr. Rodgers; but Capt. McCafferty was in favor of Camp Bello. He always had a Canadian scheme in his head. When I found this plan was being put into operation I cried bitterly, and saw that "we were sold."

Mr. Killian reported the receipts of the Brotherhood, when I was working up my plan, as about $8,000 per day. The arms at this time were coming in very rapidly. I suppose I could at that time have selected 4000 stands of arms.

Mr. Skeehan and myself stood in the relation of very good friends. I had at

that time some $10,000 or $12,000 worth of liquors, for sale of which he became my agent. I also made him an officer to take charge of all arms coming in.

The reason for putting so many officers under pay on board the Privateer was to get her out of the harbor as soon as possible. However, it would have been time enough to put three officers under pay when the vessel was ready for service.

I instructed Capt. Hodgson to order men to leave their situations for the purpose of taking service on this vessel. I think it was not injudicious, considering the finances of the Brotherhood, to place so many officers under pay as then perilling their life and limb, and the valuable services they rendered were, I consider, equivalent for the money they received.

I declined to have a civilian associated with me in the purchase of arms, artillery, &c., as I considered the military men connected with me sufficently qualified to attend to that business. A Mr. Kavanagh was named by the Central Council to take part with me in these purchases, &c., to which I objected.

I never heard that Mr. Stephens sent positive orders that no expedition should leave until he should come to America. However, I think no movement should be made without consulting James Stephens, so that co-operation with him should be had. I never sent word across to Mr. Stephens that there were four steamers armed equipped ready to start for Ireland, and only waiting the arrival of a signal officer.

Any opposition I received in my efforts to have an expedition start for Ireland came, I judged, from the Treasury Department, presided over by B. D. Killian. Col. O'Mahony, I felt then and now firmly believe, co-operated with me in all my movements, and gave me all the assistance in his power to bring what movements I had under way to a successful close.

I sent the Central Council an approved roll of the naval officers I employed, at the same rate as the next grade below in the U. S. Navy; one half to be paid in cash, the balance in bonds of the Irish Republic. There full rate of pay to commence when the funds of the Brotherhood would warrant, and they went into active service.

REPORT OF GEN. MULLEN (NAVAY DEPARTMENT, F. B.) APRIL 2, 1866

No.	Name	Rank	Weekly Pay	Remarks
1.	R. M. Hodgson	Capt. & Eng'r in Chief	53.84	These officers are all
2.	Alphonse Barbot	Captain	53.84	under pay, and have
3.	Haurahan, Thomas	Captain	53.84	been paid up to March
4.	M. D. Hickey	Commander	43.07	31st, 1866.
5.	John Powell	Commander	43.07	
6.	J. F. Kavanagh	Commander	43.07	
7.	Francis Henderson	Chief Engineer	43.07	
8.	William Hanion	Lieutenant	28.84	
9.	Peter O'Connor	Lieutenant	28.84	
10.	William M. Swann	Surgeon	28.84	
11.	Michael Moss	Second Assist't Engineer	23.08	
12.	John Earl	Second Assist't Engineer	23.08	
13.	William Lawless	Third Assist't Engineer	19.25	
14.	James F. Crummy	Carpenter	19.25	
15.	James Crawley	Carpenter	19.25	
16.	Timothy Ford	Third Assist't Engineer	19.25	
17.	Henry Tuomey	Mate	19.25	
18.	Henry O'Neill	Boatswain	19.25	

No.	Name	Rank	Weekly Pay	Remarks
1.	James P. Ralph	Ensign	23.08	These officers have been
2.	Thomas Gavaghan	Second Assist't Engineer	23.08	examined by the Naval
3.	Thomas Walsh	Lieutenant	28.84	Board, and found qualified
4.	Thomas Monks	Mate	19.25	for the positions opposite
5.	Daniel O'Keeffe	Second Assist't Engineer	23.08	their respective names.
6.	John Breen	Boatswain	19.25	They are not under pay,
7.	Patrick Culnane	Surgeon Steward	15.00	but ready for duty at a day's notice.

Respectfully submitted,

R. M. HODGSON,
Capt. and Engineer in Chief F. B.

Respectfully forwarded to Head Centre F. B.

B. F. MULLEN,
Sec'y of Military and Naval Affairs.

"THE REPORT.

At the Convention of the Fenian Brotherhood of the Department of Manhatten represented by the officers of 132 circles of the said Department, held at their Hall, 814 Broadway, April 29, 1866."

(Ten men were chosen as a committee to investigate the Fenian Government at Moffat Mansion on Union Square.   The ten men gave the following report.) :

"Brothers your Committe appointed to examine into the affairs of the F. B., as conducted at Headquarters, 32 East 17th street, would most respectfully report, that after a diligent inquiry and searching investigation, they find that the general

(page 48)

administration of affairs has been conducted in a most reckless and criminal manner."

(The committee found that the executive officer, Head Centre, Col. John O'Mahony was guilty of gross mis-management in financial and military affairs and incompetant in leadership of the F. B.)

"All warrants for payments by the established rules of the organization, required the approval of the Head Centre, and in every instance received it, proving Mr. O'Mahony's unfitness as a financial and executive officer; and nearly all, if not all the frauds thus perpetrated on the Brotherhood by various officials at Headquarters were indirectly the result of this incapacity, imbecility and total unfitness of the Head Centre for the resonsible and honorable position to which the respect and confidence of the Brotherhood had exalted in him."

(page 49)

"The Military Department has been one of the curses of the institution; and that the management of affairs undre General B. F. Mullen, Secretary of War, etc. was of the most reckless and extravagant character.   An expensive and useless staff was employed, drawing large salaries, and performing no legitimate duties.   In addition thereto, many of them drew compensation and expenses for organizing, so called.

The mis-management of no Department did more towards sapping the foundations of the Brotherhood than the Military Bureau, whose plans of action were entirely non-commenserate with the funds in the Treasury."

(page 49)

"The Organizers (paid speakers) of the F. B. were an expensive appendage to the organization, and the labors they performed were far below the large amounts drawn from the Treasury for their maintenance.   As a body they were of no benefit; on the contrary, from their incapacity, peculiarly and particularly prominent, were an injury to the cause.

The Central Council was, in reality, the great canker worm of the Brotherhood;

(page 50)

and had there been no such institution, or had men of integrity, capacity and pure patriotism taken part in its sessions, we should to-day have been far advanced on the "war path" of Irish Liberty."

(page 51)

"The entire cost of the Campo Bello expedition was over $26,000, money drawn from a treasury at that time almost depleted.   This sum was expended on an experiment, which has since entailed disgrace and disaster upon the cause, arising entirely from criminal mis-management of the leading officials who ordered it. The Committee have made every effort in their power to throw light upon this affair and they find, from the evidence here adduced, that its disasterous failure was caused in a great measure by the want of co-operation of the parties at headquarters with those having military conduct of affairs at Campo Bello.

(signed)   EXECUTIVE COMMITTEE."

STATEMENT OF CAPT. COLSON, OWNER OF THE SCHOONER NAMED THE
"TWO FRIENDS" USED AT EASTPORT, AND EVENTUALLY SCUTTLED.

I was employed by B. D. Killian to be ready at all times to transport, men,
arms, &c., and for which I was to receive $10 per day. This pay for the use of my
schooner, one man and myself. I was paid up to the 18th of April. Then Mr. Killian
left and I received orders at headquarters from Mr. P. A. Sinnott and others to
continue and be prepared to transport some men and provisions to Lubeck. I got
ready, and on the night of April 22d, fifty to sixty men came down the wharf with
several cases of muskets. When I saw this I jumped on the wharf and refused to go.
At this time it was a dead calm. A pistol was put to my head, and I was forced on
board. The men put the muskets, provisions, &c., on board, then ordered me to steer
for the island of Campo Bello. I endeavored to comply, but there being no wind we
drifted towards the British fleet, at anchor a few miles below. The men kept below
and remained very quiet. We drifted past the British fleet, but so close to them
that the watch on deck could look down on us and see everything on the deck of my
schooner. This was a trying moment for the brave men below, and, although my
schooner was forced into this service, I made up my mind to sink with them before I
would be captured by the English fleet. After we had drifted past, I observed more
English vessels a distance below. Not wishing to run any unnecessary risk, I went
below and consulted with the men. They concluded that it was best to get over into
American waters. I got one of the men on deck, and we used three sweeps and pulled
until we got out of British waters. We then ran to Allan's Island. The men consulted among each other and they determined to capture Campo Bello,* if every man
should lose his life in the attempt. We then sailed from Allan's Island with a
fair wind, but was soon apprised that the English war boats were in pursuit of us.
We then strained every nerve to keep ahead, but they gained on us rapidly. After
we had rounded a point of land we saw a large schooner under full sail coming up the
bay. The men ordered me to lay along side of her. I did so. They sprang on board,

<u>revolvers in hand</u>, and captured the schooner.   I then asked them to let me depart,
but I was told to get on board the large schooner.   I refused.   A pistol was put
to my breast.   I had to obey.   Some men went on board of my schooner and sunk her.
I could not tell why they sunk her but afterwards I saw it was to deceive the British
boats in pursuit of us, for they passed us and hailed the man at the wheel and asked
if he saw a small schooner going towards Campo Bello.   He said yes; she had just
rounded a point of land two miles below.   They passed on; we put on all canvas and
made for the American side, where we arrived safe, saving arms, provisions, &c.   My
statement will be vouched for by all the men.   I worked 13 days at $10 per day, for
which I received but $20 leaving $110 due me at present.   I lost my schooner, which
cost me $500, which was every dollar I was worth in the world.   I am now without
a dollar to pay my way home, nor have I anything to support my family.   I now come
to you, asking you to consider my embarrassment and remunerate me for the loss of
my vessel.

(Signed)

CAPT. COLSON,

Owner of the Schooner,"Two Friends."

It was moved and carried that the matter of Capt. Colson be referred to the
Brotherhood of the Department of Manhattan at their next public meeting for their
action.

May 8, 1972

Synopis of Col. B. F.
Mullen's Activities
as Secretary of War
of Military and Naval
Affairs, New York Irish
Republic(Fenian Brotherhood)
as found in the April 1866, "A full and complete report of the
investagation of the management of affairs, financial, military
and civil, of the officials at the Fenian headquarters
(Moffatt Mansion) Union Square, New York; Statement of monies
received and expended, bonds issued, — full history of
the'Campo Bello' Fizzle." Col. Bernard F. Mullen was
Secretary of Military and Naval Affairs from about January
to April of 1866. His own personal testimony covers pages
30-37 of the above mentioned report.

1) Col. Bernard F. Mullen was a General in the Fenian Army.

2) Col. O'Mahony's Testimony, pages 8-9
    "There have been, and are, too many persons on board the
privateer under pay, but I was afraid to discharge them.
General Mullen became offended because civilians were to be
associated with him in the purchase of all munitions. Mr.
Hodgson was rated as Chief Engineer by General Mullen at
of J. J. Rogers."
    Col. O'Mahony's Testimony, page 11
    "General Mullen, shortly after organizing our Department,
sent out to Ireland a detailed plan of operations on a grand
scale and requested that a Signal Officer to be sent from
there here, to arrange matters so our fleet could be recog-
nized. The"organizers" in the aggregate did not add largely
above expenses to the Fenian funds, however, I do not think
the system of organizing did harm in the Manhatton District."
"There were four boats bought for the Campo Bello affair.
They cost $300."

3) Re-Examination of Col. O'Mahony, page 17
    "I believe, sir since the inauguration of the New Consti-
tution, there has been a continuous attempt to prevent the
sending of money to Ireland. The Senate did it, by creating
offices. Then Gen. Mullen began his lavish expenditure. I

have since been convinced that if General Mullen was not a
traitor, he was almost one. I have a letter from a British
spy in Brooklin, asking money to buy a suit of clothes, and
pay passage to Washington, so as to appear before Sir Fred-
erick Bruce, and another letter to this spy from Mr. Bruce,
advising him to join the F. B., thus showing a desire to join
the Brotherhoood for sinister purposes.(Copy of letter here
shown)."

4) Captain Richard Norris Testimony, page 18 — May 3, 1866
"The Military Convention held lately in New York at
which I was present, and a member, was convened by order
of and presided over by Gen. B. F. Mullen and approved by
Col. O'Mahony. General Mullen proposed for each and every
one to go directly to Ireland, which was agreed to by a
majority at this Convention. The Campo Bello movement was
never mentioned at this Convention. The only movement other
than on Ireland was, that on telegraphing certain signals over
the wires, certain iron vessels which General Mullen gave us
to understand were owned by us would move from the Pacific
coast on an objective point. Since the Convention General
Mullen admitted personally to me that there never were any
such vessels on the Pacific coast."

5) Col. Kelly's Statement, page 20
"I heard no mention made there of any movement on Canada
or Campo Bello. I was never consulted in respect to the
Campo Bello movement. I was not admitted to the sessions of
the Central Council until the C. B. movement was arranged.
The plans of Gen. Mullen at the Convention were unanimously
endorsed. General Mullen demanded, I think $89,000 as the
amount necessary to start to Ireland with. He said that the
Central Council refused to give him the money and thwarted
his plans. He(Gen. Mullen) designed moving about the 17th
of March. He stated he would go on one ship to the western
coast of Ireland, and Col. O'Mahony on another ship to the
southern coast. I always believed in the sincerity of Gen.
Mullen up past the middle of March, when Mr. Killian said, he
(Gen. Mullen)should have the money. About that time I com-
menced to lose my confidence. I think no man at the Military
Convention doubted General Mullen's sincerity. I think a
movement on Ireland at that time could have proved successful.

SOCIETY OF THE PRECIOUS BLOOD

ST. CHARLES SEMINARY

CARTHAGENA, OHIO 45822

2a) Col. O'Mahony's Testimony, page 10
"The Eastport affair is the cause of the present
falling off of the Brotherhood. The appointment by the
Department of Manhattan I believe will be beneficial,
and meets with my approbation. I did state publicly
that the privateer was out to sea, for I relied on Gen.
Mullen's statement. It was intended to have sent the
privateer out when the Eastgate affair took place. I
think even now she can be sent out."

5a) Col. James Kelly's Statement: page 20
"I am the Inspector- General of the Fenian Brotherhood;
was a member of the Military convention; held the same
position then I now hold. There was no special committee
of that body for the arrangement of plans, etc. Gen.
Mullen submitted his plans, and the Convention acted on them."

                                        page 20
"(By Col. T. J. Kelly, Envoy from Ireland.) I received
a letter from Gen. Mullen when I was in Ireland stating
that a fleet was ready to sail, and the co-operation of a
signal officer from Ireland was necessary to prevent the
hazard of disaster. In accordance with that, I am now
in this country. "We have on hand -- " etc.(list ofarms
bottom page 20 & top of page 21.)

     B. Doran Killian's Examination resumed,   page 42
10)   " the cause of General Mullen's resigning was that
I refused to give him money in advance for purchasing cannon,
&c.   Col. O'Mahony promised to have placed in Eastport
Bank to my credit $10,000. It was not done. I received
no money except $550, which was my own private funds, until
the 11th of April, when I considered the chance of a
successful movement over, and then only $5,000. I had no
money while in command essential to pay for the provisions,
tools, implements, &c. that were necessary to be purchased."

The cause of the failure was according to General Mullen's statements to me, the non-appropriation of the money by the Central Council. I received an order for the shipment of arms from Col. O'Mahony(order shown) on the afternoon of the 3rd of April before 4 p.m. of April 4th they were aboard the vessel and receipted for. I heard Gen. Millen state that he was waiting for signal officers to come from Ireland."

page 20-21 continues giving a list of munitions and arms, at the bottom of page 21.
"Had the plans of the Military Convention been put in force, it could have been carried out faithfully to the letter by at least three of the officers in this building. The Central Council, as General Mullen said, was the power that opposed its execution, as they possessed full control and power in this matter."

page 22
"I stated in writing that I considered the place on Pearle Street unsafe. We hired by General Millen's authority, a store on Washington street, but Gen. Mullen would not have it, because the F. B. could not obtain full control of the building. I considered the charges of the carmen for the removal of arms exorbitant, and very often refused to pay the bills."

6) Re-examination of Captain M'Cafferty, page 24
"Gen Mullen asked for the fighting plans of Stephens I told him Mr. Stephens did not intend to send his plans to America, to have the battle fought on this soil. He would, when properly supported, fight it out on Irish soil. General Mullen stated in the Military Convention that by the seventeenth of March he would be ready to go on one ship with 25,000 stands of arms and 400 or 500 officers, and land on a certain part of the coast of Ireland."

page 25
The Head and Centre was to go on another ship with a 25,000 stand of arms and the same number of officers. I discussed the Signal question with him, and he agreed to send Capt. Earbot a naval officer(late of the Confederate navy) of

culture and experience to England immediately. On my return
trip I found Capt. Barbot here and General Mullen excused
himself on the ground that he knew of some cannon hidden
under ground down South and wanted Capt. Barbot to find it.
I then ordered Gen. Mullen in the name of James Stephens, to
send another party who had been selected to Europe, as an
Envoy. I then went to Washington and on my return found that
the party was still here. Walking down the street one day
with J. J. Rogers, he said to me, "Captain; we must keep
our eyes opened; we are being swindled."

page 25 of the report
    "He openly charged that between Mr. Killian, Gen.
Mullen and Pierce Skehan, the Fenian Brotherhood had been
swindled out of $1,000. He was talked down; but Mr. Rogers
kept up his cry until Mr. Skehan came and paid $500, and
admitted that General Mullen allowed him $500 as commission
for buying the privateer. General Mullen denied the power
of the Central Council to appoint a civilian to accompany him
or his staff in the purchase of war materials. Gen. Mullen
was in the liquor trade and Pierce Skehan was his agent.
At times several thousand stands of arms were in jeopardy,
and were saved only by threats of public exposure etc.."

7) Vouchers of Jeremiah Kavanagh, page 26
    "My endorsement was necessary on all vouchers before
they were paid, but B. D. Killian, at the request of General
Mullen, on account of my refusing to endorse vouchers without various items accompanying, had my endorsement on some
of General Mullen's bills dispensed with, and thereby prevented dishonest bills from being properly and carefully
investigated and audited. Bills for extra services of
and staff of General Mullen were presented to me, and I
refused to audit them because these men were being paid a
regular salary of $3 per day, and all legitimate expenses.
They were allowed an extra compensation of $2 per day, thus
realizing over $5 per day. The orders for this payment were
endorsed by General Mullen and Mr. Killian. It is my belief
that Mr. Killian allowed this extra claim in order to secure
the sympathy and support of these men, and thus purchase
their silence in regard ot the Eastport expedition."

Statement of Mr. Griffin Treasurer of F. B., page 28
"Whilst absent, I received a dispatch from Col. O'Mahony saying: -- "Come home immediately; can't do without you.' Advantage was then taken of my absence to rush some bills through which I would have refused payment. I objected to a bill being paid to Gen. Mullen, amounting to $600, presented to me without vouchers. B. D. Killian ordered it paid, stating that Gen. Mullen would forward details on return. Gen. Mullen got six hundred dollars from me to establish an agency for sale of bonds in Philadelphia."

page 29 of the report
"Mr. Wynne(Dist. Centre of Philadelphia) protested against drawing of said amount of money from the Treasury for this purpose. Mr. Wynne stated that he gave Gen. Mullen five hundred dollars as a gift to the cause, on the representation of Gen. Mullen(which have since proved false) that he had several war vessels and twenty thousand stand of arms."
--- Mr Giffin resuming etc..---
"I objected to the payment of the six hundred dollars because I knew the Philadelphia men did not desire it. When General Mullen returned to New York he did not hand any money to the Treasury -- on the contrary he desired more. Complaints were often made by the officials here that I was a tough customer because I insisted on a knowledge of idems in bills before paying them. "" — etc."
"Yesterday in a conversation between Col. O'Mahony, Mr. Kavanagh and myself, in regard to the Privateer, and he(Mr. Kavanagh) expressed his desire and intention of passing over the vessel to the Brotherhood. General Mullen borrowed of Mr. Wynne, District Centre of Philadelphia, one hundred dollars and the F. B. made it good to Mr. Wynne. Gen. Mullen promised to pay it back to Mr. Wynne, but I told him to pay it back to the Fenian Treasury. I saw a letter from a Mr. Devine, stating that he had loaned Mr. Meany, the District Centre of Ohio, one hundred dollars from the Fenian funds. (Thus these men, in their official capacity borrowed and used Fenian funds for their private use.)"

** Historian's note** The above testimony was given on May 5th, 1866.

9) <u>Col. Mullen's Statement</u>, page 31 (major excerpts)

"My position in the F. B. was Secretary of Military
and Naval Affairs. I held that office about three months."
— (He goes on to name the members of his staff & their
salaries.) — "I was about to purchase two batteries and
had made all arrangements for the purchase of one of them,
but could get no money to do it. The Central Council
prevented its purchase. My staff received extra compensation
for services as Organizers &c, in addition to their regular
pay. I think that they were of great benefit to the Brotherhood. Capt. Hodgson was not an Organizer. I do not consider
it was unpatriotic for salaried officers to charge expenses
of public meetings. I do not think that the F. B. could
have done without my staff. There is only one vessel belong-
ing to the Naval Department of the F. B.. I did not depend
so much on voluntary donations of arms as on those offered
for sale. I never set a particular day for moving." —
(He goes on to mention his plans and the propositions made
at the Military Convention.) — bottom page 30 & page 31
General Mullen made arrangements for the purchase of the
privateer for the Fenian Brotherhood. According to Gen.
Mullen the Privateer actually only cost $29,000 — and not
the quoted $30,000. —
        "I never heard of the Campo Bello movement until it
took place. The Campo Bello or any other Canadian movements
were not discussed or alluded to at the Military Convention
of which I was the chairman. My plan was to dispatch one
vessel to the north, commanded by myself, to the north of
Ireland, and the H. C. was to go to another point in Ireland
in a second vessel both to be supplied with plenty of arms."
—(General Mullen now talks about the Central Council)—
        "I sent a requisition for $89,000 to carry out this
plan, but I never heard from it again. 'Mr. Killian tried
to be Secretary of War as well as Secretary of the Treasury.'
The Central Council also tried their hands at military
matters. I then sent in my resignation as Secretary of War
of the F. B.." — General Mullen then presented to the
Committee a copy of his letter of resignation.

Note** page 37 contains the official — "Report of Gen. Mullen
(Navy Department F. B., — April 2, 1866) This report deals
with statistics — and is not to be given here.

9a) General Mullen's letter of resignation, pages 32-35
He gives a very good defense of his actions based on
the Fenian Constitution — and feels that he has been
betrayed by the Central Committee. — In regard to the Campo
Bello movement: "In my oppinion no movement should be made
of a military character unless the project is submitted to
the best military talent in reach of the Brotherhood." —
"The members of my Staff are as devoted to the cause of
Ireland as any set of men alive. They are soldiers of prac-
tical experience, and men with courage." — "Why not submit
military movements for their opinion? Can it possibly do
harm? These are the questions I put for a calm reflection."
"From all the foregoing you see how impossible it is
for me to act in my present position any longer with any
credit to myself or of benefit to the cause, therefore I
respectfully insist upon the acceptance of my resignation.
                Faithfully and fraternally yours,"
                        "B. F. Mullen"
9b) page 35 — General Mullen's Examination continued:
General Mullen among other things admits — "Mr. Skehan
and myself stood in the relation of very good friends. I
had at that time some $10,000 or 12,000 worth of liquors for
sale of which he was my agent..I also made him officer to
take chargeof all arms coming in." (objects to civilian
helping in the purchasing of arms etc.) — "I declined to
have a civilian associated with me in the purchase of arms,
artillery, & etc. as I considered the military men connected
with me sufficiently qualified to attend to that business. —
A Mr. Kavanagh was named by the Central Council to take part
with me in the purchases,&c., to which I objected. — "I never
heard that Mr. Stephens sent positive orders that no expedition should leave until he came to America. However I think
no movement should be made without consulting James Stephens,
so that co-operation with him should be had. I never sent
word across to Mr. Stephens that there were four steamers
armed and equipped ready to start for Ireland, and only waiting the arrival of a signal officer. — (next he mentions)
"Opposition in my efforts to have an expedition start
for Ireland came, I judged from the Treasury Department presided over by B. D. Killian. Col. O'Mahony, I felt then and
now firmly co-operated with me in all my movements and gave
me all the assistance in his power to bring what movements I
had under way to a successful close. I sent the Central Council
an approved pay roll of the naval officers I employed at the
same rate as the next grade below in the U.S. Navy; one half
to be paid in cash, the balance in bonds of the Irish Republic.
Their full rate of pay to commence when the funds" would warrant.

10)   B. Doran Killian's Examination resumed, page 42
"The cause of General Mullen's resigning was that I
refused to give him money in advance for purchasing cannon
etc.."

11)   Under the title of Report of the Commission, page 49
"The Military Department has been one of the curses of
the institution; and the managment under General Bernard F.
Mullen, Secretary of War etc., was of the most reckless and
extravagant character. An expensive staff was employed,
drawing large salaries, and performing no legimate duties.
In addition thereto, many of them drew compensation and
expenses for organizing, so called."

12)   A True Copy of Minutes of the "Central Council" with
      Regard to the "Campo Bello" Movement, page 63
      C. C. assembled:
      Present   John O'Mahony, H.C.
                     James J. Rogers
                     P. H. Sinnott
                     J. Kavanagh
                     Capt. McCafferty, Proxy for Tobin
                     Col. Halpin
      The Cabinet also entered into joint session:
      Present   Col. B. F. Mullen, Secretary of Mil and
                                          Naval Affairs
                     B. D. Killian, Financial Secretary
                     P. J. Downing, Secretary of Civil Affairs
      "The resolution of Mr. K. was offered and but withdrawn.
Moved by Sinnott that H.C. appoint one of the Cabinet officers
to occupy Campo Bello in accordance with the understanding
that Mr. Stephens does not arrive before next Monday.
            Ayes: Nays:
            Killian   Rogers
            Sinnott   Halpin
            McCafferty   Mullen
            Kavanagh

                     H.C. reserves decision

13)   Headquarters Fenian Brotherhood, page 64
      "The Central Committee assembled — April 2, 1866
Letter from Colonel Mullen dated: March 31, 1866 received
and read."

14)   Vouchers, Bonds and Salaries where Gen. Mullen is mentioned
      pages 69-94
      a) Voucher 157 to R. M. Hodgson(Naval Affairs) Officers
      salaries, one week, $53.43 and 28 per week ... $3.25
      Signed,   R. M. Hodgson, Capt. &
page 69   B. F. Mullen   Engineer in Chief
      b) Salaried Officers of the Fenian Brotherhood
      General B. F. Mullen — Military — $1,500 per year
page 82
      c) Organizing Special — Jan. 10th 1866
page 84   War'nt 15 — Gen'l B. F. Mullen — $102.15
      d) Mar. 21st, 1866 — expenses to Philadelphia
page 85   War'nt 61 — Gen'l B. F. Mullen — $50.00
      e) Jan. 22, 1866 — Gen'l B. F. Mullen — $5.00
page 85   War'nt 4
      f) Privateer(Col. Mullen's ship) — $30,000, page 86
      g) Mar. 13, 1866 — Gen'l B. F. Mullen
page 86   War'nt 5 for Frank McLean   — $90.00
      h) Jan. 22, 1866 — Gen'l B. F. Mullen — salary on account
page 88   War'nt 7 -Military Affairs Acc. $222.00
      i) Jan. 24, 1866 — Gen'l B. F. Mullen — 12 muskets
page 88   War'nt 10 for John Vaughn   —$60.00
      j) Jan. 26, 1866 — Gen'l B. F. Mullen
page 88   War'nt 12   — $51.89
      k) Feb. 28, 1866 — General B. F. Mullen
page 88   War'nt 30   — $117.05
      l) Feb. 28, 1866 — General B. F. Mullen
page 88   War'nt 31   — $189.00
      m) Mar. 9, 1866 — Gen. B. F. Mullen
page 89   War'nt 34   for Pilots   — $142.00
      o) Mar. 10, 1866 — Gen. B. F. Mullen
page 89   War'nt 35   for Department Force $33.00

14) Vouchers, Bonds Salaries continued, pages 69-94

page 89	p) Mar. 10, 1866 — General B. F. Mullen War'nt 36	for Department Force	$50.00
page 89	q) Mar. 20, 1866 — Gen. B. F. Mullen War'nt 62		$110.06
page 89	r) Mar. 21, 1866 — Gen. B. F. Mullen War'nt 65	for Pilots	$142.00
page 89	s) Mar. 29, 1866 — Naval Dept. War'nt 123		$100.00
	t) Mar. 29, 1866 — B. F. Mullen War'nt 125	Pilots	$142.00

u) Mar. 30, 1866   B. F. Mullen

War'nts 143 -148 For Dectective Service

B. F. Mullen		$75.00
"	" for Col. Kelly	$148.00
"	" for Col. Malcaky	$148.00
"	" for Col. Murray	$148.00
"	" for Capt. Casey	$45.00
"	" for Capt. Philip	

page 89 | | Dogherty | $45.00 |

v) Secret Service Account ** Gen. B. F. Mullen

	War'nt 7 — Feb. 28, 1866 —	$75.00
page 91	War'nt 8 — Feb. 28, 1866 —	$9.00

w) Mar. 7, 1866 — Gen. B. F. Mullen - $147.00

x) Salaries Account Continued:

Feb. 28, 1866 — Gen. B. F. Mullen

page 92   War'nt 40   - $175.00

y) Mar. 30, 1866 — B. F. Mullen Military

page 92   War'nt 133   Dept. $129.70

z) Bond Account Expenditures

Mar. 15, 1866 — B. F. Mullen on Bond

page 94   Account $600.00

Historian's note*   The complete Fenian Report is 102
pages long; reference to Mullen
ends on page 94.

**The Military Convention alluded to in this Report was
held at New York, N.Y. on Feb. 22, 1866.*

FENIAN NATIONAL CONVENTIONS

1st Nat.	Nov. 3, 1863	Chicago, Ill.
2nd Nat.	Jan. 17, 1865	Cincinnati, Ohio
3rd Nat.	Oct. 18, 1865	Philadelphia, Pa.
4th Nat.	Jan. 2, 1866	New York, N.Y.
Military Convention Feb. 22, 1866		New York, N.Y.
5th Nat.	Feb. 27, 1867	" "
6th Nat.	Aug. 21, 1867	" "
7th Nat.	Aug. 24, 1868	" "
8th Nat.	Aug. 25, 1869	" "
9th Nat.	Aug. 30, 1870	" "
10th Nat.	Mar. 21, 1871	" "
11th Nat..	Aug. 20, 1872	" "

State Convention: Indpls. Ind   Mon. May 2nd, 1864
Tues., May 3rd, 1864 " " "   "MAY BALL"

1865   Col. Bernard F. Mullen attended the 3rd Nat. Convention
N.Y. Times Index: Oct. 21 - page 2, col. 2
"The floor was turned over to Col. Mullen of Tennesse and
P. W. Dunn, of Illinois, who addressed the convention at
length. - (two from each State and District be appointed
on Government, Constitution and By-Laws, each state and
district to choose it own committemen)
TENNESSE: Col. B. F. Mullin and Martin Kerrigan"
1865   N.Y. Times Index: Oct. 24th) "elected Senators"
page 1, col. 5   "B. F. Mullen, of Tennessee

General B. F. Mullen presided over the Military Convention
of Feb. 22nd, 1866 as Secretary of War.

Benedict R Maryniak
62 Alexander Avenue
Cheektowaga,New York 14211
7/12/82

Brother Andy,

Thought I'd catch you up on my activities these past months.
I hope your silence is due to pleasant business and that my letter
finds you well.

I've been very successful in collecting data regarding the canadian
units involved at Ridgeway & Ft Erie. Private collections & public
libraries in Hamilton,Toronto, and St. Catherine's were gold mines.
I even found interviews from the 1920s featuring "last survivors" of
the Fenian Raid units. Many pictures of the personalities,too. I
am going to visit the Lundy's Lane Historical Society soon in order
to have a go at identifying some articles taken from Irish prisoners
at Ridgeway! That Society was run by a Lt Col Cruikshank in the old
days, and he was another entusiast concerning Niagara region history.

My pursuit of Archives data is slow and the expenses are scarey
due to the "unknown quantity" involved. Mr John Busey seems competent
enough (he wrote the recent book on "Regimental Strengths at Gettysburg,")
but my requests require him to roam over sep parts of the Archives.

In looking through adjutant reports from Indiana, I was able to
identify the leader of the Indiana companies as Captain James B. Haggerty
of the 13th Indiana infantry (re-organized in the field) Co. E.

Further searching of canadian papers & their coverage of the
Toronto Fenian trials, I found much on Rev John McMahon. He was about
45 years old,of stout build and medium height;he had several old
facial scars and gray hair. He was born in Ireland. He was present
at the Ft Erie raid,wearing a pistol/belt over his clerical garb - he
wore his clerical outfit to the trials,as well. Tried almost a year
after all other prisoners in October of 1867,he was found guilty,
his death sentence commuted,and finally released from jail in July of
1869. Reports on the 1870 raid into Canada mentioned him as being
there! All your info about St. Mary's Church in Anderson was confirmed
by court reporters.

After recent checking of many states' adjutant reports, the following
Civil War/US units contributed participants to the Ridgeway/Ft Erie
actions:
97th,35th,13th Indiana infantry & 5th Indiana Cavalry

15th Kentucky infantry,40th Ky Mounted Rifles,2nd Ky Cav

34th Ohio infantry

21st,49th,73rd,78th,100th,110th,164th,179th,155th NY infantry;
12th,16th,and 11th NY cavalry;and the 69th NYNG.

I've been lucky in finding a good deal of personal data on certain
leaders,although there are some maddening gaps in my collected info,
especially concerning the Tennesse & Ohio men.
Please le t me know how you're doing........

Indiana detachment to the IRA - originally 100 men in two co.s   I-Indianapolis

Balfe,John: F Col not in raid (Promoted. Lt.Col, 35th Ind. Regt, 1st Bn - Canton)
Bouler,Thomas: MC;I
Bywater,John: MC;I

Casey,Dennis:MC;Anderson
Curran,Patrick: MC;I
Casey,Thomas: MC;I
Cloughlin,Dennis: Anderson;MC;

Driscoll,William:MC;I
Dunn,John:MC;Anderson
Dempsey,John: MC;I
Delaney,Patrick: MC;Terre Haute
Dougherty,Patrick F: MC;I
Dalton,Nicholas: MC;I
Drummond,William R:MC; Terre Haute

Fitch,John M: MC;Terre Haute

Galigan,John:MC;Terre Haute
Garry,Charles:MC; I
Griffin,Michael: MC;I
Grancy,Dennis:MC;I
Green,Joseph: MC;I
Cogan,Richard:MC;I

Hudson,Luther: MC;Terre Haute
Hagerty,James S: F Captain;MC;
Jones,John: MC;I
Johnson,Joseph: MC;Anderson
Kelly,John: MC;I
Kennedy,John:MC; Parkersburgh
King,Dennis: MC; I